THE BIGGEST BED IN THE WORLD

by Lindsay Camp
illustrated by Jonathan Langley

Collins

An imprint of HarperCollinsPublishers

For all the children who've ever slept with a foot in my ear. L.C.

For Toby, Holly and Rosita who all loved the 'big one bed'. J.L.

Also by Lindsay Camp:

The Midnight Feast illustrated by Tony Ross
Billy and the Barglebogle illustrated by Peter Utton

Also by Jonathan Langley:

Snore! by Michael Rosen
Where Are You Hiding Little Lamb? by Hiawyn Oram
Collins Nursery Treasury

First published in Great Britain by HarperCollins Publishers Ltd in 1999
1 3 5 7 9 10 8 6 4 2
ISBN: 0 00 771119 0
Text copyright © Lindsay Camp 1999
Illustrations copyright © Jonathan Langley 1999

When Ben was a baby, he liked
to sleep in his mum and dad's bed.

At first, it was fine.

But, as Ben grew bigger, the problems began.
"How am I supposed to sleep like this?" said Ben's dad.

Ben's dad tried sleeping in Ben's bed,

but that was even worse.

So Ben's dad went to the furniture shop

and bought a bigger bed.

At first, it was much better.

But then...

Ben's baby brother Billy was born.

"How am I supposed to sleep like this?" said Ben's dad.

So he went back to the furniture shop and bought the biggest bed they had.

At first, it was a lot more comfortable.

But, then...

the twins, Beth and Bart, were born

and the problems began all over again.

"Oh no!" groaned Ben's dad. Then he had an idea.

He went and bought a lot of wood, and took it upstairs.

Then he fetched his tool-bag, and hammered and crashed and banged until he'd built...

the **biggest** bed in the world.
It was enormous! It was so big, he had to knock down
several walls to make a bedroom big enough for it.

"There," said Ben's dad, putting down his hammer. "Now, at last, I should be able to get some sleep."

And he was right.

The bed was big enough for all the family to sleep comfortably.

Even after the triplets, Briony,
Bella and Boris, arrived.

But the biggest bed in the world
was also the heaviest bed in the world.
And knocking down the walls had
made the house rather weak and wobbly.

So, in the middle of the night...

Faster
and
Faster
until...

Down
Down
Down

went the bed.

SPLA

"Ow!" said Ben's dad. "How am I supposed to sleep like this?"

After that, Ben's mum and dad went back to sleeping
in an ordinary bed.
And Ben's dad banned Ben and Billy, and Beth and

Bart, and Briony, Bella and Boris from creeping into it.
"Now I'm sure to get a good night's sleep," he said.
But do you think he did?

No. The ordinary bed was a very nice bed, and very comfortable too. But somehow, it seemed...
well, a little empty.

Ben's dad lay awake, tossing and turning, for hours.

" How am I supposed to sleep like this?" he moaned.

"I'll never get to sleep."

But in the end, he did.